The Most Beautiful Tree in the Forest

To Katie —

Happy Storytime

Joy Jackson McHugh

The Most Beautiful Tree in the Forest

by

Joy Jackson McHugh

illustrated by

Dorothy Hall B. Torres

Kinder House Publishing

For my grandchildren

Katie, Jeffrey, Erin, Randy,
and all future grandchildren.

- With love -

Once upon a time there was a tree in the forest. She was dressed in beautiful green leaves and rich brown bark. Her lines were straight and tall.

"Oh, I'm so beautiful," said the tree every day. "Oh, what beautiful leaves I have. Oh, how straight I stand."

There was a sparkling pond in front of her with crystal-clear water. The pond created a mirror for her to look into all day long and admire herself. "I can't believe it. I'm the most beautiful tree in the forest," she would say every time she looked into her pond mirror.

There was a row of evergreen trees, all girls, in back of her. The tree would laugh at them when she saw their reflection in the pond mirror. "You girls are so ugly. You only have needles where I have beautiful leaves. You don't have rich brown bark as I have, or lovely branches. You're kind of fat and I am slim. You are a horrible color, as well. Oh, how I admire myself."

The evergreen trees told her not to be so conceited and cruel. "You'll be sorry some day," they chanted. "Oh, ha, ha," said the tree. "You are all jealous of me."

One day a bright-eyed brown squirrel came running by the tree. "This is a nice place to make my home," she said. "I will just chew some of the tree's bark to make a nest, then I will bring my squirrel babies here to live." She began to chew the tree.

"Stop right now!" shouted the tree. "Get out and go away! I am too beautiful for you to touch me." She screamed so loudly that she frightened the poor little squirrel away.

The evergreen trees heard and saw all this. "You are very cruel and selfish. Some day you'll be sorry," they warned.

"Don't talk to me," the tree said. "You are all jealous of me."

The tree continued to admire herself in the pond mirror as she swayed to and fro in the warm breezes. "Oh, how graceful I am. How beautiful I look," said the tree.

The next morning, the tree felt something heavy on her top branch. She also heard loud chirping. "That can't be a messy, dirty old bluejay," she said. "Oh, my heavens, it is! Stop making all that noise and stop fluttering your wings. In fact, get off my branch! I am too beautiful for you to touch me."

She shook her branches with such force that the startled bluejay fell to the ground and became so frightened he just hopped away.

The evergreen trees saw and heard all this. "You are very cruel and selfish. Some day you'll be sorry," they chanted.

"Don't talk to me," the tree said. "You are all jealous of me."

The tree swayed in the warm breezes and hummed and admired herself in the pond mirror. She fell asleep, contented, until loud laughter awakened her.

Three little children were laughing, singing and dancing around the tree. "I'll bet I can climb this tree higher than you can," said one of the children. "Let's have our picnic first," said another. "I think I'll pick some of the tree's leaves," said the third.

The tree was very upset. "How will I get rid of the children?" she thought. "They are too noisy and they might make me ugly." She started to shake and sway and some of her tender branches fell on the children's heads.

"Oh, what's happening?" said one of the children. "Maybe we should move and have our picnic by the pond." They ran away.

The evergreen trees saw and heard all this. "You are very cruel and selfish. Some day you'll be sorry," they cried.

"Never talk to me again!" said the tree. "You are all jealous of me."

The tree spent the rest of the summer admiring herself in the pond mirror.

The evergreen girls did not dare talk to her. The animals, birds and children would not go near her.

"I am the most beautiful tree in the forest," said the tree.

Fall came, and with it the weather became cool and damp. The sun stayed behind the clouds for days at a time. The night brought the frost creeping from the lonesome meadow to the forest trees. The tree felt strange as she watched her lovely leaves turn from green to yellow.

One morning she looked into her pond mirror and saw a frightful sight. Her beautiful leaves were now a horrible brown color. They were twisting and twirling to the ground. Piles of dried leaves lay at her roots.

"If this continues I will be ugly and bare," she said. "Oh, evergreen girls, help me. What is happening to me? You look beautiful. You still have your thick green needles."

The evergreen girls smiled and spoke softly. "We told you that some day you would be sorry for treating everyone so badly. Being mean and selfish really hurts everyone! You must promise to be kind in the future. Promise and maybe some day you will be beautiful again."

"Oh, I promise. I promise," said the tree.

She stood under the dim starlight every night. The moon reflected her ugly, bare sight in the pond mirror. The tree was so ashamed, she hung her head and cried.

Time passed. It became winter. The snow was falling like feathers from the sky. The soft flakes came down silently until they completely covered the forest.

The cold north wind never stopped blowing. Long shiny icicles hung from the tree's bare branches. The tree shook because she was so cold and lonely. "If only a squirrel or bird were with me to keep me company," she thought. "Oh, I promise, I promise to be kind and good. Oh, what have I done!"

The tree stood frozen as the snow continued to fall. Weeks went by slowly. It seemed like winter would never end. Then, one day, she saw and felt something change.

A cloudless sky looked down on her, and the forest was bathed in golden sunlight. The cold north wind stopped blowing, and the snow was slowly melting.

Warm southern breezes drifted into the cool, thick forest. Young flowers were poking their heads up through soft green grass that was sprouting everywhere. The forest became alive with chirping birds, and the animals began to scamper around. Spring had finally arrived!

The tiniest buds were appearing on the tree's branches. A few weeks later, she was in full bloom. Delicate, light green leaves swirled around her branches. Rich brown bark lined her trunk. She could see her reflection in the pond mirror and was so excited. She was beautiful again, but this time beauty and kindness also flowed through her branches.

The birds and animals throughout the forest heard her calling to them. "Please come visit me," she said. "Come make your home with me."

Now that the tree was friendly and loving, the animals, birds and children weren't afraid of her anymore. The evergreen girls watched in joyful silence.

The birds began to build their nests on her high branches. The squirrels brought their squirrel babies. Children came to play and have their picnics under her welcoming leaves. Her branches were extended in loving friendship. The tree was so proud. She was the happiest tree in the forest, for now she shared her beauty with everyone.

The evergreen girls were proud of her, and happy too, for their dearest wish had come true. "Now, you are truly the most beautiful tree in the forest," they all chanted.

The tree had learned a valuable lesson, and the forest became a happy, peaceful place to live once again.